FIGURES in Art

Words that appear in **bold** type are defined in the glossary on pages 28 and 29.

Please visit our web site at: www.garethstevens.com
For a free color catalog describing Gareth Stevens Publishing's
list of high-quality books and multimedia programs, call
1-800-542-2595 (USA) or 1-800-387-3178 (Canada).
Gareth Stevens Publishing's fax: (414) 332-3567.

Library of Congress Cataloging-in-Publication Data

Baumbusch, Brigitte.
    Figures in art / by Brigitte Baumbusch.
      p. cm. — (What makes a masterpiece?)
    Includes index.
    ISBN 0-8368-4379-7 (lib. bdg.)
    1. Human beings in art—Juvenile literature. I. Title. II. Series.
N7625.5.B38   2004
704.9'42—dc22   2004045383

This edition first published in 2005 by
Gareth Stevens Publishing
A World Almanac Education Group Company
330 West Olive Street, Suite 100
Milwaukee, Wisconsin 53212 USA

Copyright © Andrea Dué s.r.l. 1999

This U.S. edition copyright © 2005 by Gareth Stevens, Inc.
Additional end matter copyright © 2005 by Gareth Stevens, Inc.

Translator: Erika Pauli

Gareth Stevens series editor: Dorothy L. Gibbs
Gareth Stevens art direction: Tammy West

Printed in the United States of America

1 2 3 4 5 6 7 8 9 08 07 06 05 04

FIGURES
in Art

by Brigitte Baumbusch

033117

GARETH**STEVENS**
GS
PUBLISHING
A World Almanac Education Group Company

What makes a figure . . .

Jean Dubuffet, a French painter, drew brightly colored **figures** with just a few lines, the way children do.

These two little figures are signs that were used in **ancient** Chinese writing, two to three thousand years ago. They look like human figures, but they probably stand for words or letters.

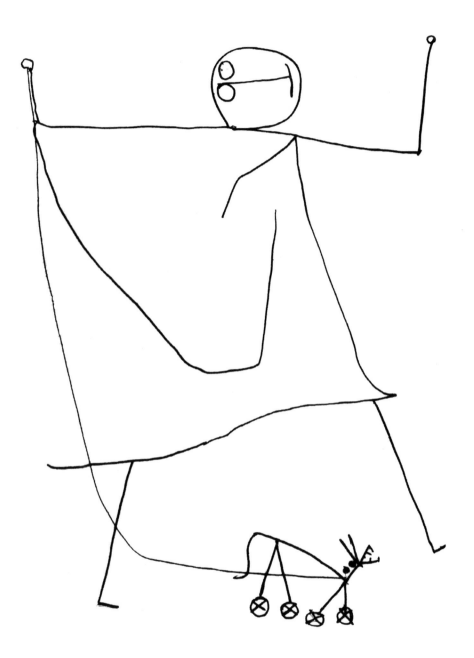

This little girl with her toy animal is a simple line drawing done in 1939 by Swiss artist Paul Klee.

a masterpiece?

A figure can be a piece of wood.

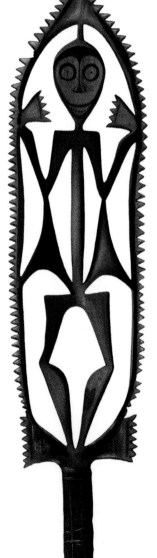

The African artist who made this figure used a branch that already looked like a person sitting down.

Some of the people of the South Sea islands have dances during which they wave wooden poles. Each pole has a funny looking carved figure at the top. This monkeylike figure (right) is from New Britain, which is an island of Papua New Guinea.

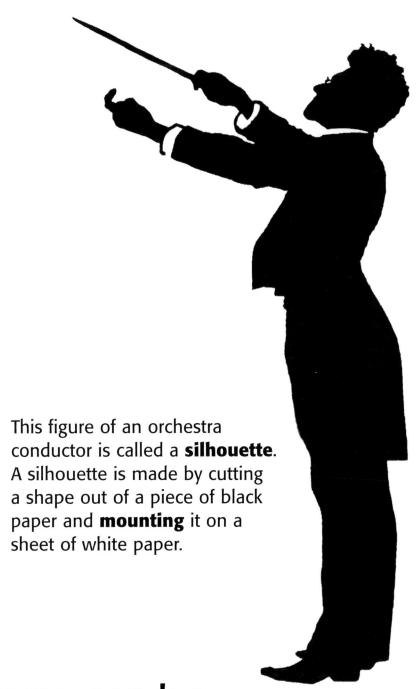

This figure of an orchestra conductor is called a **silhouette**. A silhouette is made by cutting a shape out of a piece of black paper and **mounting** it on a sheet of white paper.

A figure can be
a piece of paper.

A figure can be made of clay . . .

These **crêche figurines** are painted **terra-cotta**. They come from the South American **Andes** and are dressed just like the Indians who made them. The Christ Child is in a type of pouch that is still used in South America for carrying small babies.

or iron.

This large iron figure represents the god of war of the Yoruba tribe. It might also be the **blacksmith** god who taught the Yoruba how to work iron. The Yoruba are an **ethnic** group in the West African country of Benin, which was previously known as Dahomey.

Figures can be huge...

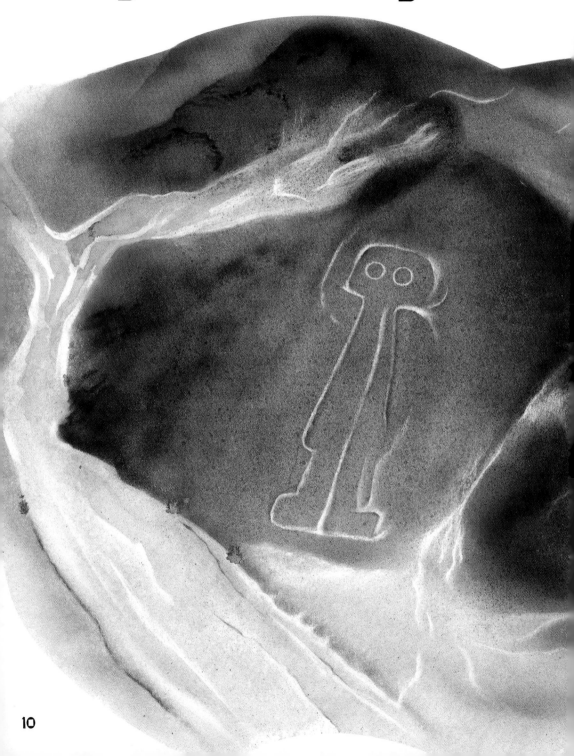

or tiny.

This huge outline of a human figure is on an **arid** hillside in Peru. It has been on this hillside for over a thousand years. The figure was drawn by making grooves in the ground.

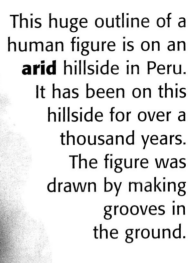

By comparison, this Egyptian **statuette** is tiny. It is only 8 inches (20 centimeters) high. A figure in the shape of a **mummy**, like this one, accompanied a **pharaoh** to his **tomb** so the pharaoh would have servants in the next world.

Figures can be as thin as a rail...

This bronze "rod" was made by the Etruscans who lived in Italy before the Romans.

or as round as a ball...

This terra-cotta "ball" was made in Sardinia.

Both of these figures come from Mediterranean countries and are approximately the same age — about 2,300 years old.

An Italian artist drew this scene of men fighting more than four centuries ago. The figures are made in cube shapes, which make them look like **mannequins** or robots.

or made of cubes.

Some figures are in scale.

To show how the various parts of the human body related to each other in size, Leonardo da Vinci, one of the greatest artists of the **Renaissance**, drew this figure of a man set into both a circle and a square.

In the early 1900s, American artist Lyonel Feininger painted a long thin man and a short fat man walking along a street.

Others are out of scale.

Figures can be people by themselves . . .

This little figurine was made in the ancient land of Sumer, in Mesopotamia (now Iraq), about 4,500 years ago. The husband and wife figures are holding hands, perhaps to pray in a temple.

Early in the 1900s, Russian artist Kasimir Malevich painted this garden crowded with children playing together.

or with many others.

Figures may run . . .

Four women, running as fast as they can, were painted, in **prehistoric** times, on a rock in Australia.

In this painting from the early 1900s, there is only one little girl running, but her movement is repeated over and over, like the **frames** of a film. The artist was Italian painter Giacomo Balla.

or sit still.

This bronze statue is "The Thinker," one of French **sculptor** Auguste Rodin's most famous works. It is a figure of a man sitting, deep in thought. Rodin created "The Thinker" more than one hundred years ago.

Figures dance.

Both of these figures seem to be dancing the same dance, but one figure is much older than the other.

The dancing figure at the top was made by a French woman named Niki de Saint Phalle, in 1965. The other dancer was painted on a rock in the Sahara more than 8,000 years ago.

Pulcinella figures play on a swing. (Pulcinella was a masked clown in **Neapolitan** comic theater.) This scene was painted by Italian artist Giandomenico Tiepolo, who lived in the eighteenth century.

Figures play.

Figures sit down and talk.

French artist Paul Gauguin painted the large picture to the right more than one hundred years ago, when he was living on the South Seas island of Tahiti.

Like the women in Gauguin's painting, the two figures below are sitting and talking. They were drawn almost 10,000 years ago on a rock in Chad, which is a country in Africa.

Figures lie down and sleep.

This "Sleeping Lady" made of terra-cotta
was found in a temple on the island of Malta.
She is more than five thousand years old.

German artist Erich Heckel painted a **portrait** of his friend Pechstein, who was also an artist, asleep on a chair outdoors. The portrait dates back to 1910.

GLOSSARY

ancient
relating to a time early in history, from the earliest civilizations until about the time of the Roman Empire

Andes
the longest mountain range in the world, stretching 4,500 miles (7,240 kilometers) from the Central American country of Panama to Cape Horn, at the southern tip of Argentina

arid
extremely dry; without enough moisture or rainfall to support the growth of most kinds of plant life

blacksmith
a worker who forges, or forms, iron by heating the metal, then pounding it into different shapes with a very large, heavy hammer

crêche
a grouping of figures representing the Nativity, or birth of Christ, which includes at least one man (Joseph), one woman (Mary), and one baby (Jesus), arranged in a scene that is often set inside a small stable

ethnic
related to a group of people who share a common culture, race, or national heritage and, often, the same language, religion, or way of life

figures
shapes, forms, or outlines that represent people, animals, or objects either in two dimensions, such as a drawing, or in three dimensions, such as a statue

figurines
small, decorative, statuelike figures, usually made of china, pottery, wood, or metal

frames
the individual pictures or images on a strip of film, which when run through a projector, look as if the figures and objects in them are in motion

mannequins
forms shaped like life-size human figures, usually used by tailors or dressmakers or to display clothing on sale in stores and shops

mounting
attaching to a supporting background for display purposes

mummy

a dead body that has been preserved using the embalming methods of ancient Egypt, which included wrapping the body tightly in many layers of cloth strips

Neapolitan

related to, or an inhabitant of, Naples, which is Italy's third largest city, located on the country's southwestern coast

pharaoh

an ancient Egyptian ruler

portrait

a picture, photograph, or painting of a person, which usually shows just the person's head, neck, and shoulders

prehistoric

belonging to the time of the world before written history

Renaissance

a period of European history, between the Middle Ages (14th century) and modern times (17th century), during which learning flourished and interest in classical (relating to ancient Greek and Roman civilizations) art and literature was renewed, or "reborn"

sculptor

a person who creates works of art by carving, modeling, or molding materials such as wood, stone, clay, or metal into three-dimensional figures, such as statues

silhouette

the basic outline of a figure, most often the full length or a portion of a human body, which is cut out of a dark material, then mounted on a light background

statuette

a statue that is usually small enough and lightweight enough to be held in the hands

sumptuous

luxurious or magnificent and, generally, very costly

terra-cotta

brownish-orange earth, or clay, that hardens when it is baked and is often used to make pottery and roofing tiles

tomb

a chamber or vault, often underground, that is used as a burial place for a corpse (dead person)

PICTURE LIST

page 4 — Jean Dubuffet (1901-1985): Random Site with Four Figures, detail, 1982. Paris, Musée National d'Art Moderne. Photo Photothèque des collections du Mnam/Cci. © Jean Dubuffet by SIAE, 1999.

Two ancient Chinese ideograms from the Chou dynasty, 1st millennium B.C.

page 5 — Paul Klee (1879-1940): A Child Again, pencil drawing, 1939. Bern, Kunstmuseum, Paul-Klee-Stiftung. Museum photo. © Paul Klee by SIAE, 1999.

page 6 — Seated figure carved in a forked branch. Art of the Suku people of the Kwango River area (Democratic Republic of the Congo). Tervuren, Royal Museum of Central Africa. Drawing by Lorenzo Cecchi.

Top part of a dance staff from New Britain (Melanesia, Oceania). Private property. Drawing by Lorenzo Cecchi.

page 7 — Silhouette of composer-conductor Gustav Mahler (1860-1911).

page 8 — Crêche figurines in painted terra-cotta. Folk art of the Andes Indians, northern Argentina. Madrid, Museum of Decorative Arts. Drawing by Lorenzo Cecchi.

page 9 — Iron sculpture of a god of weapons and war or the divine blacksmith, custodian of the art of iron working. Art of the Yoruba people (Benin). Paris, Musée de l'Homme. Drawing by Roberto Simoni.

pages 10-11 — Anthropomorphic "geoglyph." Nazca civilization, 3rd to 4th century A.D. Nazca Pampa (Peru). Drawing by Lorenzo Cecchi.

Figurine in faience (glazed earthenware) of a mummiform ushabti. Egyptian art of the Late Period, c. 1000 to 700 B.C. Paris, Louvre. Drawing by Lorenzo Cecchi.

page 12 — Votive terra-cotta figurine. Sardo-Punic art, 4th to 3rd century B.C. Cagliari, Archaeological Museum. Drawing by Lorenzo Cecchi.

Small bronze staff of an officiating priest. Etruscan art, 3rd century B.C. Rome, Museum of Villa Giulia. Drawing by Lorenzo Cecchi.

page 13 — Luca Cambiaso (1527-1585): Group of Cubic Figures. Florence, Uffizi, Gabinetto dei Disegni. Photo Scala Archives.

page 14 — Leonardo da Vinci (1425-1519): Scheme of the Proportions of the Human Body. Venice, Academy. Photo Scala Archives.

page 15 — Lyonel Feininger (1871-1956): The White Man, 1907.

Private property. Photo Scala Archives. © Lyonel Feininger by SIAE, 1999.

page 16 — Anavyssos Kouros. Greek art, 6th century B.C. Athens, National Museum. Photo Scala Archives.

page 17 — Diego Velazquez (1599-1660): The Young Infanta Margarita. Madrid, Prado. Photo Scala Archives.

page 18 — Gypsum statuette of a couple. Sumerian art, mid 3rd millennium B.C., from Nippur. Baghdad, Iraq Museum. Drawing by Roberto Simoni.

page 19 — Kasimir Malevich (1878-1935): Children. Moscow, Pushkin Museum. Photo Scala Archives.

page 20 — Painting of four women running. Prehistoric rock art, Unbalanja (Australia). After a copy by Charles P. Mountford.

Giacomo Balla (1871-1958): Girl Running on a Balcony. Milan, Gallery of Modern Art. Photo Scala Archives. © Giacomo Balla by SIAE, 1999.

page 21 — Auguste Rodin (1840-1917): The Thinker. Paris, Rodin Museum. Photo Scala Archives.

page 22 — Niki de Saint Phalle (1930-2002): Nana, c. 1965. Buffalo,

Albright-Knox Art Gallery. Museum photo. © Niki de Saint Phalle by SIAE, 1999.

Painting of a dancing female figure. Prehistoric rock art, 7th millennium B.C. Tassili-n-Ajjer (Algeria). After a copy by Jean Dominique Lajoux. Drawing by Roberto Simoni.

page 23 — Giandomenico Tiepolo (1727-1804): Pulcinella on a Swing. Venice, Ca' Rezzonico. Photo Scala Archives.

pages 24-25 — Painting of two people talking. Prehistoric rock art, 8th millennium B.C. Ennedi (Chad). After a copy by Gérard Bailloux. Drawing by Roberto Simoni.

Paul Gauguin (1848-1903): "Ta Matete" (At the Market). Basle, Kunstmuseum. Photo Öffentliche Kunstsammlung Basle/Martin Bühler.

page 26 — Terra-cotta sculpture known as Sleeping Lady. 6th millennium B.C., from the hypogeum of Hal Saflieni (Malta). Valletta, National Museum. Drawing by Lorenzo Cecchi.

page 27 — Erich Heckel (1883-1970): Pechstein Asleep, 1910. Private property. Photo Joachim Blauel/Artothek. © Erich Heckel by SIAE, 1999.

INDEX